FOR THE KING

JENIKA SNOW

FOR THE KING

By Jenika Snow

www.JenikaSnow.com

Jenika_Snow@Yahoo.com

Copyright © June 2018 by Jenika Snow

First E-book Publication: June 2018

Photographer: Wander Aguiar

Cover model: Fabian Petrina

Photo provided by: Wander Book Club

Editor: Kasi Alexander

Cover Design: Designs by Dana

ALL RIGHTS RESERVED: The unauthorized reproduction, transmission, or distribution of any part of this copyrighted work is illegal. Criminal copyright infringement is investigated by the FBI and is punishable by up to five years in federal prison and a fine of $250,000.

This literary work is fiction. Any name, places, characters and incidents are the product of the author's imagination. Any resemblance to actual persons, living or dead, events or establishments is solely coincidental.

Please respect the author and do not participate in or encourage piracy of copyrighted materials that would violate the author's rights.

NEWSLETTER

Want to know when Jenika has book related news, and giveaways, and free books?

You can get all of that and more by following the link below!

* * *

Sign Up Here: http://eepurl.com/ce7yS-/

* * *

For The KING

Willow. Flower shop owner and commoner.

I was her king, a ruthless and brutal ruler who didn't back down.

And from the moment I saw her I knew she was mine. I had to have her, not just in my bed but also by my side. As my queen.

So I had her taken from her home and made a deal with her. I'd make sure her ailing mother was taken care of and pay off her debts if she agreed to one thing.

Be my wife and carry my heir.

What I wanted I got, and the only thing that I wanted more than all the riches and jewels in the world was her. Willow.

Warning: Get your fancy clothes on—or off depending on how you roll—and get ready to dive into one hell of a royal love story. It's got everything that presses your book buttons: a safe read that's swoony, filthy, and delivers a HEA. It's true what they say about this king ... he does always get what he wants.

CHAPTER 1

King Victor

"With all due respect, Your Highness, I don't think it would go over very well if we took her from her home and demanded she marry you."

I clenched my teeth and turned around, staring at Frederick, who looked at me like he should have kept his mouth shut. He should have. Hell, I was about to go over there myself and tell Willow that she was mine, that she had been mine for the last year.

From the moment I saw her in the market a year ago, standing behind her flower stall, the scent of the fresh flora not masking the fact that she smelled the sweetest, I knew what I had to do. All I'd wanted to do was throw her over my shoulder and take her back to my bed, parting those sweet thighs and claiming her as mine.

I hadn't been with a woman for years, well before I saw Willow and wanted her in my bed, my life, and by my side. Years I'd been celibate, focusing on ruling my kingdom, making it grow, protecting it.

But now it was time for me to be happy, have a family. I wanted all of that with Willow. Only her.

But I'd bided my time, waiting until I had everything secure, could make sure when she was brought to me that everything would go according to plan. She wouldn't deny me, her king, her ruler, but I wanted her to desire me the way I did her. I didn't want to keep her as a prisoner; even though I would because letting her go was not an option. I'd waited long enough to make her mine, had been more patient than I ever had before.

What I wanted I took. But the only thing I wanted in this fucking world was Willow. Crown be damned, she'd be mine.

The time had finally come for me to take a wife—Willow—and put my heir inside of her.

* * *

Willow

I DIDN'T KNOW what I was doing here—amongst these

lavish, grand items. This was the first time I'd ever been inside the palace and it was just as magical as I'd envisioned. I was a simple shopkeeper, selling fresh cut flowers in the village center, barely making ends meet to support my mother and myself. With her ailing heath, working the flower shop—one she'd built herself from the ground up—was the only thing keeping the meds in stock and my mother staying comfortable.

I couldn't be away, even for this short amount of time. I was losing money, but then again, it wasn't like I could deny the king.

What he wanted he got. Always.

So when the king's men came to my stall and demanded I come with them, I was smart enough not to ask any questions.

And so here I was, a twenty-two-year-old florist, afraid of what would happen next, worried about my mother, but more nervous as to why King Victor wanted to see me … a nobody.

And amongst the uncertainty of what was going to happen I couldn't help but think about King Victor. Big and strong, powerful and brutal, he was a force to be reckoned with. Arrogant and demanding, no one dared come up against him for fear of losing. And they always did.

But what would he want with me? I had nothing to offer, which made this whole situation even more confusing and concerning.

I heard footsteps and turned around to face the massive wooden double doors. My heart started beating this frantic rhythm and I clasped my hands behind my back, trying to appear calm even though I was anything but. And then I watched as the door handle turned, the large slab of wood being pushed open to reveal one of the servants. He was dressed in black and white attire, his head bowed as he stepped aside and showed respect for the man who entered.

Everything in my body stilled, tightened as I stared at King Victor. He was an imposing man, easily over six feet tall, with broad shoulders and narrow hips. He was muscular, the white button-down shirt and slacks he wore not hiding the kind of raw power he held.

And his silver crown glinted under the light, a show of his authority.

I swallowed, this lump in my throat forming and refusing to go down. I knew I probably looked like a deer caught in headlights; wide-eyed and frightened. He stepped farther into the room, his strong, powerful arms at his sides, his focus trained right on me.

"Leave us," he said to the servant without breaking eye contact with me. Once the door was shut and we were locked in together I breathed out slowly.

Could he see how afraid I was, how nervous his very presence made me? Still he said nothing directly to me and instead walked over to a cabinet. He opened it and proceeded to pour himself a glass of scotch.

Turning around, he lifted the bottle toward me, lifting a brow, asking me without saying anything if I wanted some. When the king offered you something you didn't deny it.

I nodded even though I wasn't an alcohol drinker, and that one glass would probably make me light-headed. But to be honest I needed a little bit of liquid courage to get through whatever this was about.

Once he had my glass filled he walked over and handed it to me. "Thank you, Your Highness," I said as I took the glass, my fingers brushing against his much larger ones. Electricity shot up my arm and right to my core. I held in the shiver that threatened to escape. He stood only a foot from me, and as he drank his scotch he stared at me.

I had to crane my neck back in order to look into his face, this man so tall and strong I felt wholly feminine in his presence. I brought the glass to my mouth and tipped it back, the liquid burning as it traveled down my throat. Sputtering as I took another drink, I could see the smirk he gave me behind his glasses.

I wanted to just come out and ask him why I was here, but I didn't dare overstep the bounds. I was a mere commoner, which made this whole situation even more confusing.

"I'm sure you're wondering why I've asked for an audience with you, Willow?"

He knew my name? I was shocked to hear that,

given the fact there were many people that lived in our village. I was one amongst many. But he knew *me*?

I nodded, not able to actually say anything. I watched him, wondering what he would say next, nervous how things would play out.

"I've seen you at your flower shop, watched you smile as you hand customers their floral arrangements."

He saw me, watched me?

"For a year I came to see you daily, even if you had no knowledge that your king couldn't take his eyes off of you." Oh, God. Was this reality? "For that year I had my self-control in check, knew restraint was what I needed. But the reality was I wanted to throw you over my shoulder and carry you to my bed, tell you with my mouth, tongue, and hands that you would be mine no matter what."

I grew wet instantly, all nervousness vanishing as my desire climbed higher. "You want me as what?" I didn't know if this was stepping over lines or disrespectful, but I had to know. "You want me as what, a consort?"

He didn't speak for long seconds. But his gaze was intense, trained right on me. "My proposition is this," he said and took a step closer to me. For a moment he said nothing else, just stared at me, his gaze dipping to my lips on several instances. "I want you as my wife, to be the mother of the next in line for the throne." His face softened and it was such a strange thing to see. I'd always seen King Victor with this stern, intense expression, one that surely scared the hell out of anyone who thought to go up against him.

"I..." The lone word spilled from me but nothing else followed.

"Your mother is sick," he said matter-of-factly but I could hear genuine care in his voice. It was a strange combination, especially coming from him to a commoner like myself. "I want to bring her to the palace, want my personal physician to start looking after her."

I didn't know what to say. His offer was worth more than he'd probably ever know.

"And this is contingent on if I marry you?" I wasn't a fool.

He didn't speak for long moments. "No. If you say no to the marriage proposal your mother will still be looked after by the royal physician." My heart was thundering behind my ribs. He took a step closer and I held my breath.

"But make no mistake that if you decline my offer I'll only try harder to make you mine."

I knew my eyes were big, felt them widen at his declaration.

"There's no one else I'd rather have by my side."

"I'm a commoner."

"You're perfection."

Could he see how fast I was breathing? Did he realize what his words did to me?

"Marriage, Willow. I offer you the throne by my side, to be the mother of my children." His voice got lower, deeper. His gaze dropped down to my lips and I couldn't help but lick them, an involuntary act.

Everything in me went still. I swore even my heart stopped beating. I had no idea what to say, how to respond. "I'm nobody. You have dozens of aristocratic women to choose from." My throat was so dry, and the lump lodged in the center of it refused to go down.

He grew very serious. "None of them hold a candle to you, Willow."

I felt my eyes widen, knew I probably looked shocked. But hell, I was. King Victor wanted me? As his wife? As the mother of his children?

"Yes, Willow," he said and stepped closer, reaching out and brushing his fingers along my cheek. My skin felt hot instantly, yet a chill raced along my arms and legs. "I only want you. From the moment I saw you I knew you were mine."

CHAPTER 2

Willow

My body was numb, my mind turning a mile a minute as I stepped out of the royal car, the door shutting behind me. I turned and watched the sleek, black vehicle drive away, so out of place for the modest area I lived in.

Facing my one-bedroom home, the one I shared with my sick mother, I made my way toward the front door and stepped inside. The scent of lavender filled my head and I turned to look at the oil diffuser going off in the corner. It was my mother's favorite scent so it was on constantly, something that helped relax her. At this point anything that would make her feel better I was all for. I closed my eyes and thought about what

King Victor had said, the deal and proposition he'd made with me.

There was no question what I would do. This wasn't just about how much I wanted him, but also about making sure my mother was taken care of. Although I couldn't deny my feelings for King Victor. From the moment I first saw him as the prince, and then taking the throne as my king, I desired him like no other. There had been no one for me, ever. It wasn't just because I wanted him that I hadn't given myself to another man.

Time and opportunity hadn't been in my favor.

I set my bag down and headed to the back room, where I knew my mother would be sitting and reading. Most days that's what she did, a book in her hand and the sun streaming through the window.

I stepped into the bedroom we shared and saw her in her favorite chair, a blanket wrapped around her shoulders and a breeze filtering in through the open window. She had her feet curled up under her and a book in her lap. I once asked her why she read so much and her response was it was her solace, a way for her to escape reality. I could understand that, especially with all she'd been through. I knew all the stress she dealt with had to weigh heavily on her.

I leaned against the doorframe and smiled at her. My mother was my rock, always had been and always would be. Her sickness came in the form of an autoimmune disorder that took her strength most days.

The door creaked as it swung open slightly and my mother looked up, her glasses perched on her nose.

"Hi, honey," she said and smiled and I instantly walked over to her.

"Hi, Mom." I sat on the edge of the bed, just a few feet from her, my hands clasped together in my lap. I didn't know how to go about saying this, to tell her I made the deal with the king. She probably would be shocked I'd even had an appearance with him, but I didn't know how she'd react to the fact I had agreed to *marry* him, to be the mother of his future children.

"What's wrong, Willow?" She set her book down and leaned forward. She looked pale, with dark circles around her eyes. Over the last year she'd gotten sicker, her body frail, weak. The money I earned went toward her doctor visits and medication, but even that wasn't enough, not with our shit insurance. And I hated seeing her so sick. I wanted to do more for her, so much more.

But now I can.

"The king asked to see me today," I said softly. Her eyes widened instantly and she sat back.

"The king?" I nodded. The silence stretched on for several seconds. "What did he what to see you about?"

I swallowed the sudden lump in my throat. My nervousness wasn't the only thing I felt. The very idea that I would marry Victor, the man who I'd lusted after for as long as I could remember, excited and aroused me.

"He wants to marry me." I stared at my mother. "He wants me to be his queen, to help take care of you, make sure you get the best medical treatment possible."

She didn't respond right away but she didn't need to. I could see the worry on her face, knew she'd try and talk me out of it.

"You can't," she finally said. "Willow, sweetheart, I will not have you whore yourself out to the king to help me." She shook her head. "No, I won't have that, Willow."

"It's done," I said instantly. "And this isn't about whoring me out." I looked down at my hands. "Marrying King Victor won't be the worst thing I could do," I whispered. When my mom didn't say anything I looked up at her.

She looked at me with this strange expression. "Willow?"

I didn't know how to respond right away, so I stayed quiet for long seconds.

"I want you to be happy, not doing something because you want to protect me."

I shook my head and smiled. "It's not just about that." I wanted to be honest with her. "It's not just that," I whispered again, feeling my cheeks heat, knowing she'd be able to see my reaction clear as day. "I've wanted him for a long time." I didn't bother telling her that it was crazy to have feelings for a man so strongly, one who was my ruler, one who I'd never even personally met.

"You think you can love him?" My mother's words were out of love; I could hear it in her voice.

I looked down, not wanting to admit that I probably already did. The feelings I had for Victor might not be rational but they were real. I lifted my head and looked at her again. "Yeah, I think I can, Mom." *I think I already do.*

CHAPTER 3

Willow

My heart was thundering, this rapid beat against my ribs. I was sure it would burst right through at any moment. I had one hand held around this simple yet elegant bouquet, my other hand curled into a tight fist at my side. The gown I wore wasn't anything extravagant—surprisingly—but was formfitting and flashy compared to my standards.

The plunging neckline started at the end of my breastbone, jewels that were priceless snaking up and around my neck. Victor had picked it out, something he said he'd envisioned me in a dozen different times. I couldn't help how my entire body became warm; no doubt a blush was stealing over me. There were a few people behind me fluffing up the train, one beside me fixing my hair, and another on the other side of me adding more lipstick. I was being pampered and prepped and I felt so out of place.

And then the double doors were opened and I stood there staring down the long, ornate hallway, King Victor waiting for me at the end. Rows of bodies filled the pews, and the balcony above, curling around the entire room, was the same. People I didn't know, aristocrats and even royalty, watched me, a commoner.

I could see my mother sitting in the front pew, but as soon as I entered the room she stood, as well as everyone else. The music started playing but my heart was beating far too loud and I couldn't hear anything else.

Taking a deep breath, I walked toward Victor, everything in me strung tight. This was really my life, my reality. I was about to marry a king, become his queen, the ruler amongst the people I'd walked side-by-side with my entire life.

And before I knew what was happening I was standing at the front of the altar, looking into King Victor's eyes, knowing this moment would change my life forever. I glanced over at my mother and I actually saw happiness on her face. Could she see how this moment affected me, how this wasn't just an arrangement?

I supposed essentially it was, a proposition made to me by my king. But I cared about him, more than I probably should have given the fact I hadn't thought I'd ever be in his life.

How things had changed.

As the officiate started the ceremony everything around me turned into a blur. Victor had my hands in his, and the feeling of his thumb moving along the back of my wrist was strangely calming and intimate. Amongst these hundreds of people I felt like it just him and me sharing this moment.

He took a step closer to me and I inhaled the masculine scent of his cologne. Or maybe it was just his natural aroma, one that had me instantly wet and needy. A part of me couldn't believe I was actually going through with this, agreeing to be his and only his. But another part, one that was far stronger, kept telling me this was right.

It felt like perfection and I was right in the middle of it.

And so here I was, about to become the queen.

* * *

King Victor

She was mine officially.

I didn't wait to be "allowed" to kiss my bride. I leaned in and pressed my lips to hers, claiming her in front of the audience, letting them all know that Willow was mine and mine alone.

There was nobody else around despite the roomful of people. With Willow right in front of me, the scent of her perfume filling my head, making me drunk, I knew I'd made the right choice. Never had a woman affected me the way she did. And as soon as I'd seen her, those flowers surrounding her, that smile on her face, no other woman compared.

She was all I thought about, all I wanted. And I made it my mission to convince her to be mine, to make her see that we were meant to be together. But even though I'd thought I'd have a fight on my hands with her, trying to make her see she belonged with me, I'd seen her desire in her gaze. She stared at me, not able to hide her pleasure, her need for me. It was then that I knew she'd give in, that she'd cave and say she was mine.

Maybe it would take her time to love me, but for Willow I had all of the time in the world.

I pulled back, wanting to kiss her for long hours, to just say fuck it and do it anyway, but I knew this was all new to her. I didn't want her to be uncomfortable and with the pink staining her cheeks I could see that she was unsure of everything.

The music still played softly, the people silent as they waited for my next move. But my next move was standing here staring at my new bride, at the woman that I'd already fallen head over heels for.

I took her hand in mine and turned toward the guests. They stood and showed their pleasure from the ceremony with smiles and clapping hands. I led my wife down the aisle and up a set of stairs. Then we were standing on a balcony, staring down at the crowd gathered below.

The cheers were deafening and I turned and looked at Willow. She faced me, her head tipped back and her eyes wide.

"What now?" she asked softly, and even though the roar of our people below was maddening, she's all I heard.

"Now we start out lives together, My Queen." And then I kissed her in front of everyone, making it known, officially, that she mine.

CHAPTER 4

Willow

The wedding night

He didn't say anything, just leaned down and captured my mouth with his. A gasp left me at the feel of his powerful kiss, of his strong lips on mine, stroking, taking what he wanted.

And he was definitely taking what he wanted.

His kiss was hard, demanding. When his hands landed on each side of my face, tilting my head to the side, controlling me so that I was helpless against him, I let myself melt even further against him. I gave myself over completely. I didn't care about anything at this moment except letting King Victor have me. He was the one with the power, with the control.

Victor was every kind of bad for me, ruthless and powerful, influential and my king. But at this moment all I could think about was how his mouth on mine was doing wicked things to my body, making me feel lost, submissive.

He pushed me back and pressed his chest against mine, sandwiching me against the wall. Victor grabbed my hips, his big hands making me feel small, petite and feminine. He slid his hands down my hips toward my back, and over the base of my spine. Then he cupped my ass. For a second he just held the globes, but then he let out this low groan against my mouth, curled his fingers against my flesh and had me needy for more.

He was forceful with his actions and I assumed this was how he always was, how he got what he wanted. Victor stroked his tongue along mine, took possession of me in ways I never imagined. I was so wet, my panties soaked clean through from my arousal.

And then he was moving his hands down to grip my skirt, the material rising up my legs. The wedding "dress" I wore was made up of two sections. The skirt and train were encrusted with jewels, emeralds and sapphires that sparkled under the lighting. The top was lace with the same jewel detailing along the bust line. It was heavy, expensive. It didn't feel like something I would ever see myself wearing.

But I was no longer the flower shop keeper. I was the queen.

I didn't stop him, didn't even want to. I wanted to be naked, to give myself over fully to him.

He groaned hard against my mouth, his long, thick, and huge cock digging into my belly. It was like something snapped in him, something making this controlled man break and become an animal. He was moaning, his actions more frantic, feral. He couldn't control himself with me and I loved it, needed it.

"You like my hands on you, don't you?" I couldn't answer, couldn't even think straight. "Tell me. Tell me all the dirty fucking things you want me to do to you."

I found myself nodding because I couldn't answer, couldn't form words.

"Tell me. Admit that you want this, Willow. Admit you want your king to break in this little virgin pussy, pop your pretty little cherry and make you mine."

Saying what he wanted would only give King Victor more power. But maybe that's what I wanted? Maybe fully giving myself to this man was exactly what I needed. I'd been in control for so long, making sure everything was in place, that being with Victor meant I didn't have to do any of that but let him control the situation.

"Tell me," he demanded, his voice hard, unyielding. He grabbed onto my ass even harder, making me gasp out from the pain he caused. But the pleasure that followed was surprising, welcomed.

"You like getting what you want, don't you?" God,

was I really saying this to the king? He could have me killed for much less. But he didn't say anything, just smirked and pressed his cock against my belly.

"Fight it. It only turns me on more."

Before I knew what was happening he had my skirt all but torn off of me and curled his hand over the mound of my ass. He grabbed the edge of my panties, pulling the material taut until it gave way and was free from my body.

Victor brought the tattered material to his nose and inhaled deeply, right over the saturated part that had been touching my pussy. This low, animal-like sound came from him.

"Fight all you want … you're mine."

CHAPTER 5

King Victor

I inhaled her panties again, that sweet scent of her pussy making my cock jerk in response. I was going to tear up her pretty virgin cunt, make it mine. She'd take all of my cock as I filled her womb with my seed, putting my heir deep inside of her, making sure she was linked to me forever.

Placing my hand between her thighs again—right over her now bared pussy—I added pressure. "Your cunt tells me you like what I'm doing, that even if you're trying to be strong you know that I'm the only one who can give you what you need," I growled out low. "You're fucking soaked and it's all because of me."

I held up my hand, my fingers glistening from her wetness. "Open for me, Willow." She widened her eyes but did as I said. I slipped my fingers into her mouth, made her taste herself.

"Lick them clean."

She ran her tongue along the digits, sucking the cream off of them, and couldn't help but make a small noise in the back of her throat.

"You like it, don't you?" I said low, wanting to hear her say the words. I removed them from her mouth, took a half a step back, and dropped to my haunches in front of her, her pussy on display, my face right there, seeing it all.

"Fuck, I like that your cunt is mine now, that no one will ever fucking taste you, know how tight you are, how wet and pink you are when you're turned on."

I blew a warm breath on her pussy. I lifted my hands and framed her cunt, and pulled her lips apart with my thumbs. My groan was deep and filled with an arousal that no doubt matched hers.

"Spread your legs for me, Willow. I'm going to lick and suck at this little pussy until you come all over my face."

She did as I ordered and I gripped the back of her knee and brought it over my shoulder, having her pussy spread obscenely wide. And then I had my mouth on her cleft, my tongue parting her folds as I ate her out almost violently.

I had one hand back on her ass, keeping her pressed to my mouth as I did exactly what I wanted with her.

Squeezing the fleshy mound, I groaned against her soaked pussy at the same time I dipped my tongue into her body. Fucking her with my tongue and lips, I gently scraped my teeth along her flesh.

I lifted the hand that I had on the back of her knee and moved it between her thighs. As soon as my thumb touched her clit she came for me.

"That's it," I said against her swollen flesh as I continued to eat her out.

A low cry left her and she speared her hands in my hair and ground her pussy into my face.

"Fuck," I groaned.

I gave her pussy one last long lick, like I was sucking on a lollipop, making sure I got all of her flavor, and then I stood. I grabbed her ass again and pulled her forward, letting her feel the hard length of my erection pressed into her belly.

I pressed my lips against hers again, ran my tongue along the seam before plunging into her mouth. She no doubt tasted herself on my tongue. She moaned in my mouth and wrapped her arms around my neck. She wasn't able to stop this.

I broke the kiss and leaned back to stare at her. "I need you, My Queen. I really fucking need you." I reached down and palmed myself again, an obscene gesture, but one I couldn't stop.

"Victor," she whispered.

I was hard as a fucking steel pipe. "You want me to

fuck you? You want my big cock plowing into you, making you mine?"

She didn't answer me and it made me desire her more. "Say it, Willow. Tell me."

"Yes." She said that one word with wide eyes and a breathy tone. I smoothed my hand over her bottom lip and she closed her eyes. It was only when I reached down to unzip my slacks that she opened them again.

I rubbed myself through my slacks for several long seconds, just watching her, not moving or speaking. But then I pulled my cock out. She lowered her gaze to the monster I unleashed, the massive erection that was long and thick, no doubt the biggest damn cock she'd ever seen. The slit was wet with pre-cum, ready for her to lick it off.

"I want you on your knees." My command was rough and left no room for argument. She knew I'd stretch her so good, so much that it would hurt, but only in the best kind of way. "Don't think, just do as I say."

I was addicted to her.

She dropped to her knees. The thick jut of my cock was right in her face, the slick tip begging to be sucked, to be cleaned off. She tilted her head back and looked up at me.

"Go on," I ordered, urged her.

I could see her whole body become tense. I ran my fingers along the edge of her face, tracing her cheekbones, her chin, and moving lower so I could gently pull her bottom lip down, opening her mouth. I slipped my thumb inside.

She thought she was wrong for me, not good enough. I'd show her that to me she was the world, the only one I wanted.... the only one I'd ever have.

I took myself in hand again, stroked my cock from root to tip, and then brought the head to her mouth. "You want my dick, don't you?"

She nodded, not daring to defy me even if she did hold so much fucking power over me.

"You want to suck me off until I fill your mouth with my cum? You want me to make you gag because my thick cock is shoved in your mouth?"

Damn, I was a filthy fucking bastard.

The tip brushed against her lips, and I made her open up wide without saying a single word. She had her eyes closed and got ready to suck my dick like my queen.

She used gentle pressure at first, dragging her teeth along my length on the upstroke, and then used a hard suction on the down stroke. For a virgin she knew how to drive me insane with need.

Willow used her tongue to tease the crowned head, then moved back down the thick vein that ran on the underside. I groaned and gripped her hair as I steadied her, starting to thrust in and out of her mouth. My actions must have spurred her on because she started moving her head up and down like she wanted my cum down her throat.

I might have had her on her knees, submitting before me, but at this moment, with my cock in her mouth, Willow held the power.

I tangled my hand in her hair, keeping her head immobilized as I slowly thrust my hips in and out, shoving my dick into her mouth. "God, so fucking good, baby." She lifted her eyes, her mouth still wrapped around my dick.

I was completely focused on her mouth, at the way her lips were stretched wide around me, at how fucking sexy that looked. I tightened my hand in her hair to the point I knew she probably felt pain, but her moan told me she liked it regardless. I knew she was the right one for me, a perfect half to make me whole. And when she hummed around my cock I sucked in a stuttering breath.

"That's it, Willow. Suck my cock. Take all of it in until it hits the back of that pretty throat of yours." I groaned after I said that, feeling the suction of her hot, wet mouth increase, then feeling the resistance of the back of her throat at my shaft head. My balls rested against her chin, my cum threating to shoot out of my cock and fill her mouth. But no, I wanted to do that in her pussy.

Forcing myself to take a step back was hard as fuck, but this wouldn't be how I got off. Neither of us moved for several seconds. I was still a fucking fiend for her and would have her no matter what, in any way I saw fit, and would show her that the king owned her.

I helped her to stand, pulling her into an embrace and kissing her hard. I pulled back only long enough to say against her lips, "I need to have you in my bed, under me, your tight little cunt gripping my cock."

She stared at me, knowing I spoke the truth by the way she looked at me, her eyes wide, her need clear. "Say it." She was silent. "Say it, Willow."

"I'll be owned by the king."

CHAPTER 6

Willow

"I want you lying in the center of the bed and naked for me. I want you spread for me, showing your king exactly who owns this body ... who owns you," Victor said with a commanding voice. I was standing by the door, my hands flat on it, my body on fire. "Now strip for me. Fully."

I didn't bother trying to fight this, not just because I didn't want to, but because Victor was ruthless when he wanted something, and what he wanted was me.

I had sweat dotting the valley between my breasts and was so aroused I was shaking with nervousness and anticipation.

He was still fully dressed, which only made me feel even more exposed. He was just so big, at least a foot taller than my own five-foot-four frame. Being in the king's presence was intimating, but knowing I was now married to this imposing beast of a man had other feelings consuming me.

I started to breathe harder the longer I stared at him. He met my gaze with a dark, penetrating one. The lights were dimmed in the room, but I could see him well, could see every part of him. He proceeded to remove his clothing, his ornately tailored outfit from our wedding coming off in pieces to reveal his large, muscular body.

He started taking off more of his clothing, all the while never taking his focus off of me. He went for his slacks next, unbuttoning them, pushing the zipper down, but he didn't take them off right away. I was transfixed at watching him undress, getting more turned on by the second.

"I want that sweet ass and pussy of yours, Willow." He growled out the words. Shivers wracked my body at the sound.

He took off his crown and set it on the dresser beside him. Then he reached behind him, over his head, and took his undershirt off that way. It was so damn sexy the way he removed the material and tossed it aside. And then the chest that was revealed had my pussy clenching, my body readying itself for Victor. His arms were huge, rippling with muscles, and his upper chest was defined. His abdomen was hard, his six-pack on clear display. And the monster between his thighs was hard and pointed right at me.

All of that was wrapped up in hard, golden skin.

"You like looking at me?"

I nodded, not even about to deny or hide it. All I could focus on was his big cock jutting out at me. He moved closer to me, and I felt my heart start to pound faster, felt the perspiration on my body become more pronounced as the anticipation filled me.

"Get on the bed and turn around and let me see that ass," he ordered.

A shiver raced up my spine. I did as he said, and when I was on my belly I looked over my shoulder. Victor was on me in the next second, running his tongue up the length of my spine, having me bow my back ... having me on the precipice of begging for him to fill me with his huge cock.

God, I felt so drunk right now despite the only glass of wine I'd had at dinner. I should have had more, but with a court full of guests watching us, judging me no doubt, I'd tried to be the prim and proper queen I now was.

Everything in me was heightened: sight, smell, hearing, and even touch. The sheets beneath me felt rough against my overly sensitive flesh.

He moved back and cool air moved along my body.

"Look at this ass," he said, but it was uttered low, so softly that it was as if he spoke to himself. And before I could even contemplate what he planned on doing, he brought his big palm down on one fleshy globe. A cry of pleasure and pain left me, heat rushing to my bottom, right under my skin. Tears filled my eyes, but as that pain started to fade and warmth took its place, I felt a tingling pleasure fill me.

He brought his hand down on my ass again, not as hard as the first time, but still with enough force it had a sound leaving me. He spanked me over and over again and I was forced to curl my hands into the sheets and hold on. That's all I could do as he had his way with me.

He didn't speak as he stood behind me, spanking me until I was biting my bottom lip hard enough I tasted blood. He made small grunting noises behind me as if he were having a hard time controlling himself.

And then I felt his hands running over my ass, teasing the erotically abused flesh, smoothing the sting away and heightening my pleasure even more.

"Damn, your ass is so red, so damn perfect." He ran his tongue over my left cheek, and then did the same over my right. "I bet I made this perfect ass sensitive, didn't I?"

"Yes." I breathed out that one word.

He continued to lick at my skin, running his teeth over the curved flesh, tasting every part of me. And then he spread my cheeks. Cool air wafted along the crease of my ass and my pussy.

"Look at how juicy this little pussy is for me, all primed and ready to be stretched by my cock."

I couldn't breathe, couldn't even think straight.

"I'm going to plow through this virgin pussy, make it mine, fill you up with my seed and make you big and pregnant with my heir."

I gasped for air, closed my eyes, and felt obscene for as much as I wanted this. With one final smack to my bottom, he flipped me onto my back, my breasts shaking from the force. He started running his hand over my breasts, pulling at my nipples and having the need crest inside of me.

"Look at me, watch as your husband—your king—takes you."

I opened my eyes, not realizing I'd closed them in the first place. He had his mouth on my nipple and ran his tongue around my areola, tracing my flesh until it puckered.

"You ready for my cock, princess?"

"Yes," I said on a moan.

"Yeah, you fucking are."

Tonight the king would own me.

CHAPTER 7

Willow

Everything in me was on fire. My blood pumped through my veins, my need to fully give myself to Victor strong.

He slid his hand between my thighs, cupping my pussy with so much pressure I gripped the sheets beneath me, trying to find something to hold on to. I was so sensitive down there, so wet and swollen for him.

"Victor." I whispered his name.

"So damn juicy." He slipped his fingers through my folds, rubbing up and down. I was ready for him and didn't bother trying to pretend otherwise.

"Open more for me."

I spread my legs as wide as they would go, so much

my muscles protested. He started stroking me harder, with more pressure, more desire. One of his fingers found its way into my pussy, the long, thick digit working me from the inside out. Victor pulled the digit out and slowly slipped it between the cheeks of my bottom, rubbing the wetness all over my asshole.

I grew tense at that sensation. I'd never had a man take me, least of all back there.

"One day I'm going to take you here, My Queen."

My breathing increased as he slipped the slick finger into my ass. A few pumps into my body was apparently all he could handle because a second later he pulled it out and replaced it with his mouth. I cried out at the sudden feeling of his tongue probing me back there, fucking a spot I never dreamed would be touched. His hands on my ass, spreading the cheeks wide, kept me immobile for his erotic onslaught. I could do nothing but cry out as the pleasure grew inside of me to a tidal wave of sensation.

After long moments of him running his tongue over the puckered hole, he pulled away, gave my ass one final smack, and stepped back. I looked at him, feeling my entire body flush from my arousal.

"Fuck," he groaned. "I could get off just looking at you." He was breathing hard, his chest rising and falling viciously. He reached down and grabbed himself, palmed his cock and started stroking it from root to tip. "Beg me for my cock," he demanded, ordered. I licked my lips, wanting him desperately, but also unused to this situation. I'd never been with a man, let alone talked so obscenely with one. "Say it, Willow."

"I want you inside of me." My heart beat so hard. "Give me your cock." he was breathing so hard "Back on your hands and knees."

When I was where he wanted me—how he wanted me—he made a strangled noise and was back on top of me, his chest pressed to my back, his heat searing me. He pushed the hair off my neck, kissing the skin that was exposed, sending goosebumps along my arms and legs. Victor squeezed one cheek of my ass, and then spread my ass once more.

"I'm addicted to this ass, princess. I'm going to eat it, fuck it … own it."

I felt dizzy, a wave of desire moving through me like a freight train.

"But not tonight. The ass fucking will be for later, after I've broken in this sweet little pussy of yours." He groaned and I made a muffled noise and buried my face further into the sheets. "Your virgin slit is too much of a temptation. I'm going to spread you, stretch you, until all you feel is me."

And then the crown of his cock was placed at my entrance, a thick promise of what was about to come.

He started to push in, slow and easy, breaking through my innocence, making it his own.

A low moan left me and I closed my eyes.

"Relax. Open up that hole for me." He started to slide into my body, my lubrication making it easier even if he was so large, so thick. And then he was fully in me, his balls pressed right to my body. He didn't wait to give me time to adjust to his massive size. Victor just started moving in and out of me, easy at first, but still fucking me like I was made for him.

"Christ."

I sucked in a lungful of air. The pain was intense, the feeling of being filled taking my sanity. But as he moved into me and retreated, there was a spark of desire, a wave of pleasure. That discomfort slowly ebbed and I let go, just felt.

"Beg your king to fuck you."

"Fuck me," I said on a moan, not even caring that I'd said the words, that they were foreign to me. He was the one in charge and I loved it, got off on it.

He smacked my ass hard. I cried out, and he did it again. He started fucking me then, hard, fast, making me take all of his dick until I felt tears fill the corner of my eyes.

"Come for me, milk my cock, have this little virgin pussy sucking the cum from my balls."

My orgasm crashed through me violently.

He was crazed in his movements, pounding into my body like he owned it. *He does.*

I tightened my pussy around his pounding cock. "Yes," I cried out as another orgasm moved through my whole body. I started pushing back against him, trying to make him go deeper.

He snaked his hand up my back to grab a chunk of my hair. Victor pulled my head back, exposing my throat. I turned my head so I could see him as he came … as he got off. His gaze was heavy lidded as he watched his cock disappear into me. Sweat glistened on his hard, defined body, and I wanted to lick it all off, wanted it covering me. I'd never felt this kind of desire before, never even imagined it could be like this.

As if he sensed my gaze he looked at me and started really pounding away. Victor grunted out every time he was balls deep in me. The pleasure was never-ending. He growled before thrusting several more times into me and then stilling. His roar of completion sounded like a feral animal.

"*Christ.*" That word spilled from his mouth in a rush as he came. He braced himself on his hands on either side of me and stayed there, buried in me, breathing hard, filling my virgin pussy with his cum. And then he pulled out with a grunt and collapsed on the bed beside me.

For several long moments nothing was said. The only sound was our erratic breathing. I turned to face him, saw his eyes closed and his chest rising and falling harshly. Sweat glistened off his hard body and my mouth watered to have a taste. I was already a fiend for this man.

He looked over at me, the corner of his mouth kicking up. He had me pulled nearly on top of him then, his arm around my waist, his cock thickening, getting hard again against my thigh.

"You better get some sleep, Queen Willow, because I'm not nearly done with you yet."

CHAPTER 8

Willow

The life of royalty and luxury was not something I thought I would ever get used to. To have people wait on me hand and foot, to have them at my beck and call, was strange and unusual. I felt out of place. If I wanted a glass of water I should get up and get it myself, not have somebody bring it to me on a silver platter, which they did.

I walked over to the window and stared out at the city, the shops and buildings, lush greens that surrounded the property. It really was a beautiful and picturesque scene, and was now mine to take in at my leisure.

Although I was the queen I refused to relinquish my flower shop. It had been my mother's before I was born. I'd stay there with her when I was younger, watching her design gorgeous bouquets and flower arrangements. It had been a safe place for me and I wasn't going to let that go because I was now Victor's.

And that's exactly what I was ... his.

But I no longer worked at the flower shop and instead had my own employees. Even now that was strange to say, knowing that people worked for me.

I looked off to the right where the sunroom was located. The indoor pool looked especially blue today as the sun streamed in through the windows. And I couldn't help but smile as I saw my mother sitting on one of the lounge chairs, her legs stretched out and a book on her lap. Some things never change.

Now that she was in the care of the royal physician, no insurance roadblocks stopping her care, she was doing much better. She had color in her face and meat on her bones. And she genuinely looked happy.

Agreeing to marry Victor, to be his queen, also meant my mother would not be left alone. So she moved in with us, into the royal palace where she had her own wing, her own library filled with books from floor to ceiling. There were so many stories for her to get lost in that she'd never have a dull moment.

I felt strong arms wrap around my middle and I smiled, leaning back against Victor. I rested my head on the center of his chest and his big, strong body enveloped me. For long moments we didn't say anything, both of us just staring out the window. I could see his reflection in the glass, his silver crown sitting atop his head. Unless I was out on official business with him I didn't wear mine. It felt strange having that weight on the top of my head, the priceless accessory filled with diamonds and rubies. But Victor had grown up with this. It was all he'd ever known.

But I also couldn't deny that I felt beautiful and important when I had it on, knowing that I could help others with where I currently was at in life. And that's what I wanted to do. So working with charities, donating my time, all of that and more was what I focused on. Well, that and the insatiable appetite Victor had for me. I had no doubt that our lovemaking would get me pregnant sooner rather than later. But I supposed that was the plan.

I turned around in his arms and tipped my head back to look in his face. His amber-colored gaze was focused right on me. But then again, it always was.

Rising up on my toes, I placed my lips against his. He instantly had his hands cupping each side of my face, holding me in place as he probed the seam of my lips with his tongue, gently urging me to open. And I did so instantly.

He swept his tongue inside my mouth and moved it along mine, instantly having me wet and ready for him, needy for the things only Victor could give me. In the short months that we'd been married I found myself hopelessly falling in love with him. He was a ruthless leader if his kingdom was threatened, but a kind and gentle one as well. He cared about his people, about the ones he loved.

Pulling back, I couldn't help but smile, my lips tingling from his kiss and my heart pounding from my emotions.

"I love you," I said softly and rested my head on his chest, hearing his heart beating a steady rhythm. I'd fallen asleep to the sound many times. His hand on the back of my head was calming and secure, letting me know that he'd never let anything happen to me. We were in this together and always would be.

"I love you, Willow, My Queen." And then he just held me and it was perfection.

EPILOGUE ONE

Willow

Six months later

My hand shook as I pulled the gown across my body. I sat on the edge of the exam table, the doctor for the royal family jotting something down in a file. "You're sure?" I asked, my voice shaky. He glanced at me and pushed his glasses up the bridge of his nose, smiling.

"Positive, Your Highness." He finished writing something down and I glanced away, thinking about everything this would entail, how this would change our very lives.

Placing a hand on my flat belly, I thought about the

baby growing inside of me, and how I would let Victor know. Since our wedding night this had been bound to happen, no protection being used as he tried to get me pregnant with his heir. But this wasn't just the next royal in line for the throne. This was *our* baby—Victor's son or daughter—something I'd grown to want desperately.

"Would you like me to call in the king to break the good news?"

I shook my head. "I'd like to tell him in private, if that's fine."

The doctor nodded and smiled. "As you wish, My Queen."

He left the room and I quickly got dressed, my heart beating fast and my hands still shaking. I was nervous but excited to tell him the news.

I quickly got dressed and headed to his office, where I knew he'd be working. My legs felt like pudding and my hands refused to stop shaking. I had to clasp them together to keep them still.

The door was partially open, so I brought my knuckles down on it twice before pushing it open. Victor was leaned over his desk, has broad shoulders hunched forward as he read the file in front of him. My mouth suddenly went dry, my throat tightening. He glanced up at me, the strain on his face evident until it dissipated and he smiled. He leaned back and held his hand out for me, curling his finger inward and gesturing me to come forward.

"My Queen," he said in that deep, baritone voice that had every part of my body coming alive.

I walked over to him and he immediately pulled me onto his lap, wrapping his arms around me and burying his face in the crook of my neck, inhaling deeply.

"I could get drunk off your scent," he said and inhaled again, causing a shiver to race over my body.

I shifted slightly on his lap and looked him in the eyes. His brows lowered and I could see the confusion settle across his face. It was clear he could tell something was up. Now I just needed to find the courage to say the words.

This shouldn't have been as hard as it was, or as difficult as I was making it. We both wanted this, but I supposed now that I was faced with the reality of it, I was a little nervous.

"What's wrong?" he said and pulled me in closer, kissing me on the lips gently. He rested his forehead against mine, his fingers gently digging into my sides, keeping me close to him.

"Nothing's wrong," I said honestly. He pulled back and cupped my cheek, his thumb stroking underneath my eye. Instead of saying the words I reached up and took his hand, guiding it down to rest on my belly. It took him a moment to understand what was going on, but I could see the realization of why I'd placed his hand there filter across his face.

"A baby?" he asked but I could hear the truth in his words.

"A baby," I replied and couldn't stop myself from grinning. I placed my hand over his, which rested on my stomach still. I wanted to say it was hormones, but the truth is I was just emotional because I was so damn happy. Tears stared to well up in the corners of my eyes and I chuckled, closing them and willing myself to stay strong.

"Look at me, My Queen."

I opened my eyes and stared into Victor's, feeling my love for this man grow. Our relationship might not have started off in the most conventional of senses, with him all but forcing me to marry him, but the truth was I was glad things worked out the way they did. He was a ruthless and brutal leader to all who came up against him, but to me he was a gentle giant, treating me like the queen I now was by title.

"I love you," he said in a husky voice and leaned in to kiss me softly on the lips. "I love you too," I replied and wrapped my arms around his neck, resting my head on his shoulder.

I knew without a doubt I was his world, that he would do anything for me. And now I was having his baby. Who would've thought a commoner like me would now be standing by the king as a queen and carrying the future heir?

Life had a funny way of working out. That was for sure.

EPILOGUE TWO

King Victor

Five years later

"Papa, Papa." Asher came running up to me, his dark curls bouncing. I scooped him up and held him as I walked over toward Willow, who stood over by the gardens holding Bethany. She was already starting to show with our third child, and if I had my way we'd have a dozen more. To hear my children's laughter, see their little faces looking up to me for guidance and protection, showed me what the meaning of life really was.

Stopping beside Willow, I adjusted Asher on my hip and wrapped my arm around her shoulders, bringing her in closer. Bethany started giggling and held her arms out for me. I took the little girl in my arms, setting Asher down on the ground and watching him chase a bird before it flew off.

I wrapped my arm around Willow again and leaned in to kiss her on the neck. She looked over at me and smiled before resting her head on my shoulder. For long moments we just stood there, watching as the birds flew above, the butterflies and bees moving around the flowers in the garden.

"Crazy, isn't it?" she asked before looking at me and rising on her toes, pressing a kiss to my lips.

"What is, my love?"

"That this is where life has taken us." She looked at me and grew serious. "Who would have imagined I'd be your queen? Who would have thought I'd be standing by your side with two gorgeous children and one on the way?"

I didn't need to think about what she said to know how I thought, what I felt. "I saw it," I said honestly and turned her so she faced me fully. "I knew this would be the outcome from the moment I saw you." And then I leaned down and kissed her, knowing that for the rest of my life this feeling—my love for her—would only grow.

The End

NEWSLETTER

Want to know when Jenika has book related news, and giveaways, and free books?

You can get all of that and more by following the link below!

* * *

Sign Up Here: http://eepurl.com/ce7yS-/

* * *

ONE MORE NIGHT

By Jenika Snow

www.JenikaSnow.com

Jenika_Snow@Yahoo.com

Copyright © May 2018 by Jenika Snow

First E-book Publication: May 2018

Photographer: Wander Aguiar

Cover model: Jonny James & Rachel B.

Photo provided by: Wander Book Club

Editor: Kasi Alexander

ALL RIGHTS RESERVED: The unauthorized reproduction, transmission, or distribution of any part of this copyrighted work is illegal. Criminal copyright infringement is investigated by the FBI and is punishable by up to five years in federal prison and a fine of $250,000.

This literary work is fiction. Any name, places, characters and incidents are the product of the author's imagination. Any resemblance to actual persons, living or dead, events or establishments is solely coincidental.

Please respect the author and do not participate in or encourage piracy of copyrighted materials that would violate the author's rights.

One More Night

When my sister passed away I adopted her daughter, Dolly, and raised her as my own. We were all we had left in this world and I was going to try my hardest to make sure she never wanted for anything.

That's why I needed someone I trusted to watch over the most important person in my life. Being a businessman meant I was out of the house a good portion of the day, a necessary evil to provide for Dolly. A live-in nanny would ensure Dolly got the best care possible when I wasn't with her.

And when I saw Emma for the first time I didn't just see a caretaker for Dolly. I saw a woman who had every caveman instinct in me rising up like a primal beast. I felt possession and need for Emma the likes of which I'd never experienced before.

I didn't just want a nanny anymore, I wanted Emma … all of her.

She might think this was just another job, but

before our time was up Emma would realize she was mine and I wasn't letting her go.

Warning: Guys, this book is going to give you whiplash for how insta-crazy it is. Talk about a hero who can't keep his hands off his woman! This may look like a sugary sweet read—and it is—but make no mistake: it's filthy as hell. We have one alpha hero who instantly falls for the heroine and won't let her go. Maybe a little obsessive, but hey, that's what we like.

CHAPTER 1

Emma

"You're firing me?" I looked between my two employers, a husband and wife who had more money than I'd ever see in a lifetime. "I don't understand. Did I do something wrong?" I felt my heart start to pound harder and faster. I looked over at the infant in the highchair, Cassie, the daughter my employers had no time for. I started taking care of Cassie three months ago. Getting up with her in the middle of the night, feeding her, giving her the love her parents didn't. It was rewarding all by itself, even if it was tiring and strenuous.

"Firing is such a negative word," Morgana said, her perfectly made-up face twisting in disgust. "We like to say trying a different path."

I lowered my brows in confusion at her response. "Finding another path?" I found myself repeating.

Morgana looked over at Robert, her husband, but he looked less than pleased even to be having this conversation, as if he had more important things to do.

"We just don't feel you're a fit for the household." She shook her head slowly.

This wasn't about being a fit for the household; this was about Robert having grabby hands and Morgana not liking it. Apparently when your husband sexually harasses the help, that means you fire them. That's how you deal with the issue of your husband being a big asshole.

Maybe this was a blessing in disguise. Because it didn't matter how many times I told Robert how inappropriate his leg brushes to my arms or back were, or how I didn't appreciate the lightly laced sexual things he said to me. And all it ended up doing was having Morgana blame me even more.

"We just don't feel you're the right fit for Cassie," Morgana said, her voice and tone clipped, as if I were annoying her.

"I—I don't know what to say." I looked between the baby, Robert and Morgana, not sure what to say.

"We'll give you a day to clear your stuff out of the guest house," Morgana said, dismissing me.

I didn't say anything else as I headed toward the guesthouse. This was my second position, and although I hadn't seen myself staying here permanently, I had at least hoped it wouldn't be a temporary position like my first one was.

I moved past the pool and into the small one-bedroom house. Closing the door and leaning against it once in my room, I stared at the interior. A single bed, one nightstand, a plain dresser, and one picture of an ocean view hanging on the wall. On the nightstand there was a frame, one I'd brought from home: a picture of me and my mother, which had been taken years ago. It was right before she passed away and the only item that held any value to me.

But the room itself was sparse, especially given the extravagant detail put into the main house.

I walked over to the small closet, grabbed my bag and started packing my clothes. I would head to the agency tomorrow and look to see if they had any openings in the same area. I'd look for one with a contract, one that wasn't month-to-month like Morgana had done. No doubt she went through nannies like days of the week.

Maybe this was a blessing in disguise? I'd find something that would make me feel like an extension of the family. And to be honest, that's what I wanted. With no family aside from ones that were so distant they didn't even know who I was, I was looking for that missing piece since I'd lost my mother.

Tomorrow was a new day, right?

* * *

Jacob

I NEVER THOUGHT I'd be a father, but after my sister Raina passed away I became just that.

A two-year-old little girl had come into my life not knowing what was up or down, how to process just losing her mother, and I was her sole caregiver.

Dolly was this rambunctious little girl who'd brought meaning into my life for the last five years. And for those years I'd been her father, the one person she depended on, looked up to.

We were all we had left in this world.

Even five years after my sister's passing I could look at her little girl and see Raina staring back at me. Dolly, with her wild mane of golden locks, the curls bouncing when she ran around, was just like my sister had been when she was that age.

I'd ended up having babysitters help throughout the years. And as much as I hated the way my schedule was, that I had to have people look after her so much, I was tired of having so many people coming in and out of her life.

And so having someone live with us and be there for Dolly, making sure she had a stable environment, was a priority. I just wished I would have thought about this and done it well before now.

I looked at the website for the live-in nanny positions, knowing that this was a big step bringing someone into our lives, into our home to look after Dolly.

But with summer break coming up I needed someone who could be here with her at all times, keep her occupied, make her feel the love she deserved when I wasn't here. I didn't just want someone to babysit her. I wanted someone who could be that other figure in her life, the one she was missing out on because her mom was gone.

What she needed was a mother. But that was something I didn't know if I could ever give her. As a man focused on Dolly and work, I didn't have time for relationships. In fact, I'd been so consumed with making sure Dolly never wanted for anything, that her mother's passing didn't consume her, I hadn't been with a woman romantically for five years.

But I hadn't wanted nor needed anyone in my life like that. I'd never found anyone who was good enough for Dolly ... good enough for me. Celibacy worked just fine.

I exhaled and ran a hand over my short hair. Bringing up the nanny portfolio, I skimmed the prospective women. I don't know how long I stayed at that computer, but I was getting a kink in my neck and the eyestrain was giving me a headache. I was about to say fuck it when I clicked on the last portfolio.

The picture had everything in my body tightening. I read her details, feeling my heart start to pound a little harder, this possessive need in me rise unexpectedly.

Name: Emma Marsh

Age: Twenty-Four

Gender: Female

Education: Associates in early childhood education.

Experience: Less than one year

I continued reading about her background, how she only had two previous positions in this field, the most recent one having lasted only a handful of months before she was let go. I stared at her picture. She was smiling almost shyly, her eyes big and blue, her hair blond like sun-kissed wheat in a field. I felt everything in me tighten the longer I stared at her image, this overwhelming feeling consuming me. I wanted her. I wanted her really fucking badly. It was sheer control alone that made it so I wasn't sporting a huge fucking erection right now.

I'd set up an interview with her and pray like fucking hell she got along with Dolly, because something inside of me demanded I make her mine. It was primal, fucking insane, but it felt so right on every damn level.

I was insane, confused, but I couldn't have talked myself out of this even if I wanted to.

And I sure as hell didn't want to.

I needed Emma Marsh and everything inside of me told me to go after her.

Out Now: https://amzn.to/2KYTiX1

WANT MORE?

Find all of Jenika's dirty, sweet, and everything in-between books here:
http://www.jenikasnow.com/bookshelf

Want your very own Real Man? Check out the series
HERE: http://amzn.to/2szRFss

ABOUT THE AUTHOR

Find Jenika at:

Instagram: Instagram.com/JenikaSnow
Goodreads: http://bit.ly/2FfW7A1
Amazon: http://amzn.to/2E9g3VV
Bookbub: http://bit.ly/2rAfVMm
Newsletter: http://bit.ly/2dkihXD

www.JenikaSnow.com
Jenika_Snow@yahoo.com

Made in the USA
San Bernardino, CA
20 July 2018